by Ann Downer

illustrated by Shennen Bersani

In a world of stripes and shadows, where the seahorses played, Shark Baby was rocking, rocking in the arms of Mother Ocean, tied fast to a strand of kelp.

For a while he could do somersaults in his egg case. That was fun. But now Shark Baby was too big to turn around. Besides, he wanted to know what was outside in the wide, blue ocean.

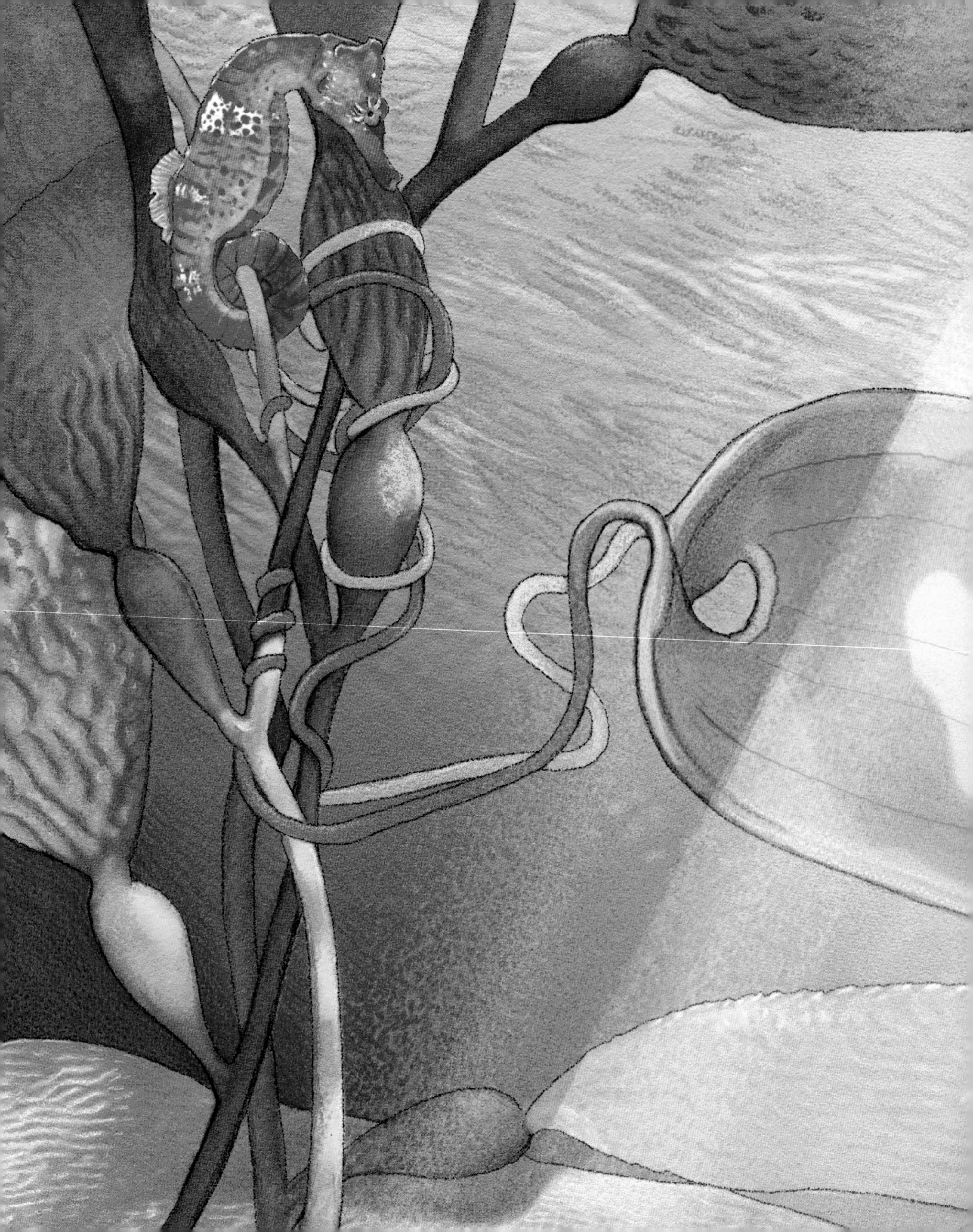

What kind of shark am I? he wondered. But squirm as he might, he could only see the tip of his tail.

He asked Mother Ocean, but she would only rock him, and say *hush, hush.*

That night Mother Ocean brewed up a storm, and she rocked that baby a little too hard.

Snap! The egg case broke loose, and Shark Baby went tumbling and rolling in the rough, wild current.

That current was cold and that current was strong! It whirled Shark Baby and it hurled Shark Baby and it roared in his ears. It bounced him off rough coral and dragged him along the sandy bottom.

But at last the wild, blue current roared itself out, and Shark Baby's egg case came to rest.

All the tumbling and rolling, whirling and twirling had made a tear in his egg case. Now Shark Baby could see! And he saw . . . spots!

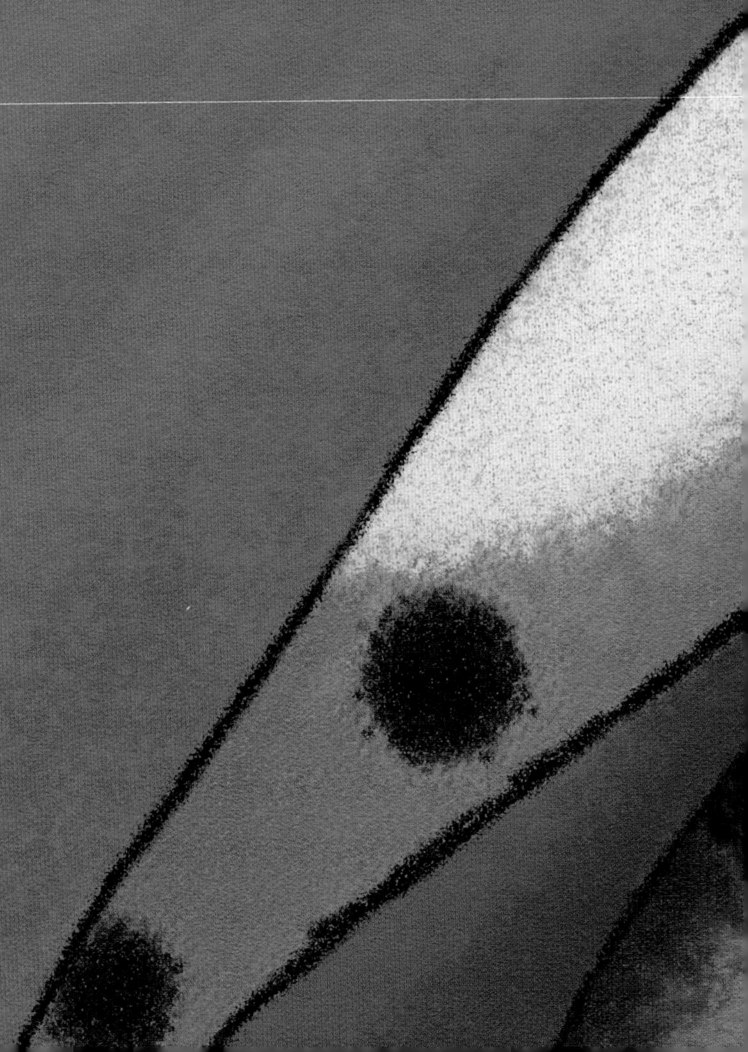

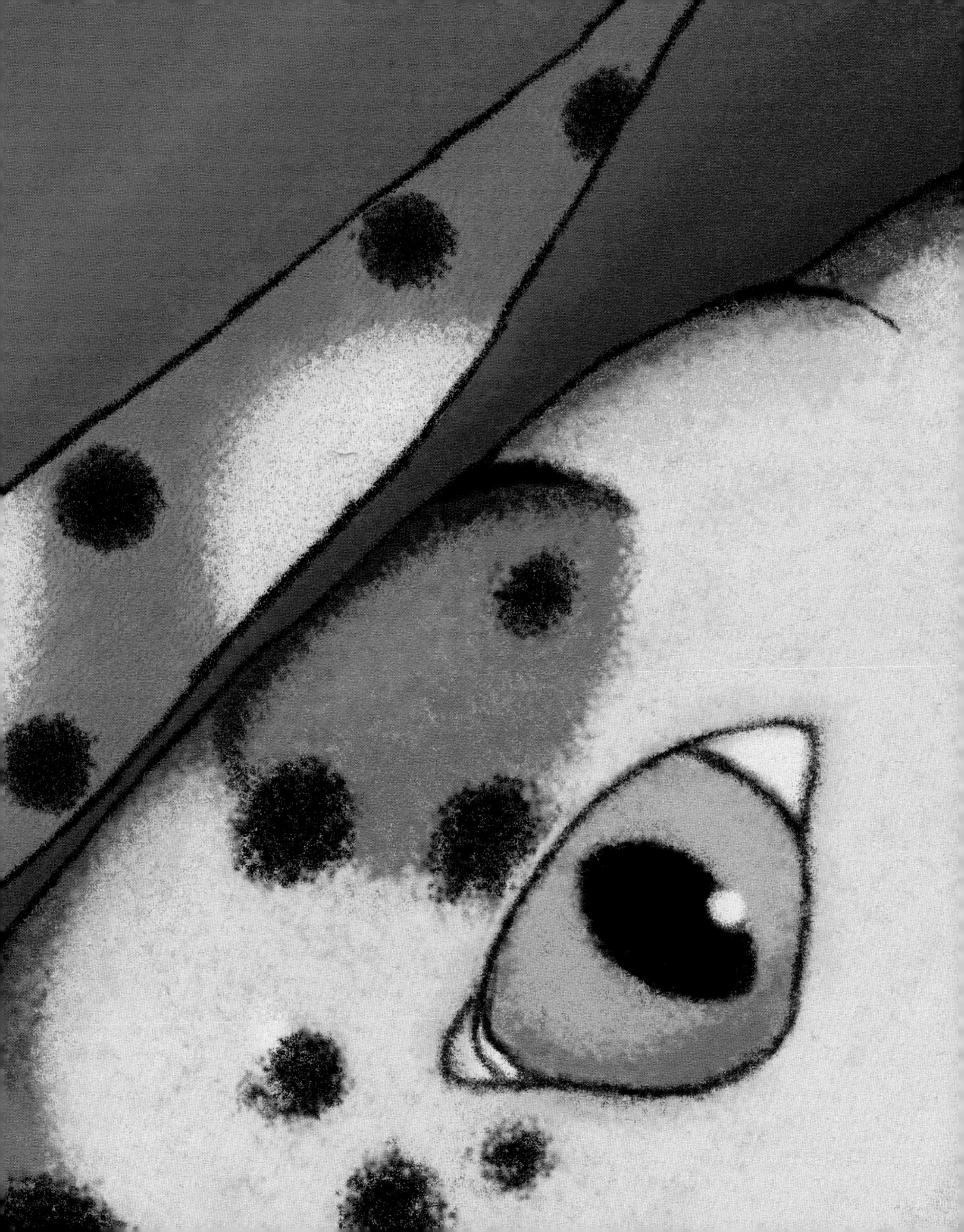

"What are you?" asked Shark Baby.

"I am a horn shark," said the spotted shark. "What are *you*?"

"I don't know," said Shark Baby. "Maybe I am a horn shark, too."

But the horn shark just laughed. "Your case is all tattered and torn. My baby has a fine spiral egg case. You are not a horn shark."

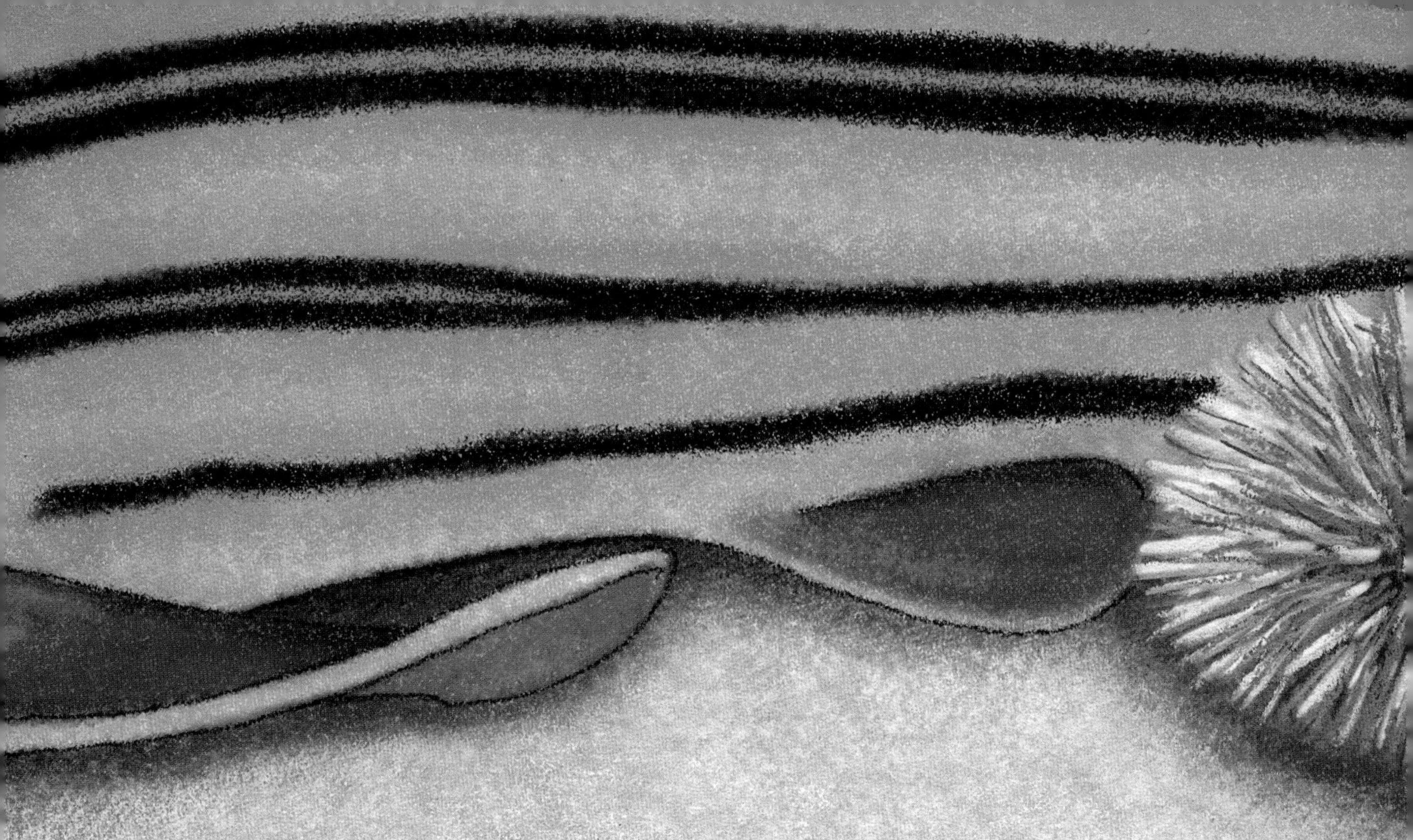

The current picked up Shark Baby and carried him on, to a garden of sea urchins on a rocky reef. He looked out through the gap in his egg case and saw . . . stripes!

“What are you?” asked Shark Baby.

“I am a pajama shark,” said the shark, showing off his stripes. “A pajama shark is a fine thing to be. What are you?”

“I’m a pajama shark, too,” said Shark Baby. “At least, I think I am.”

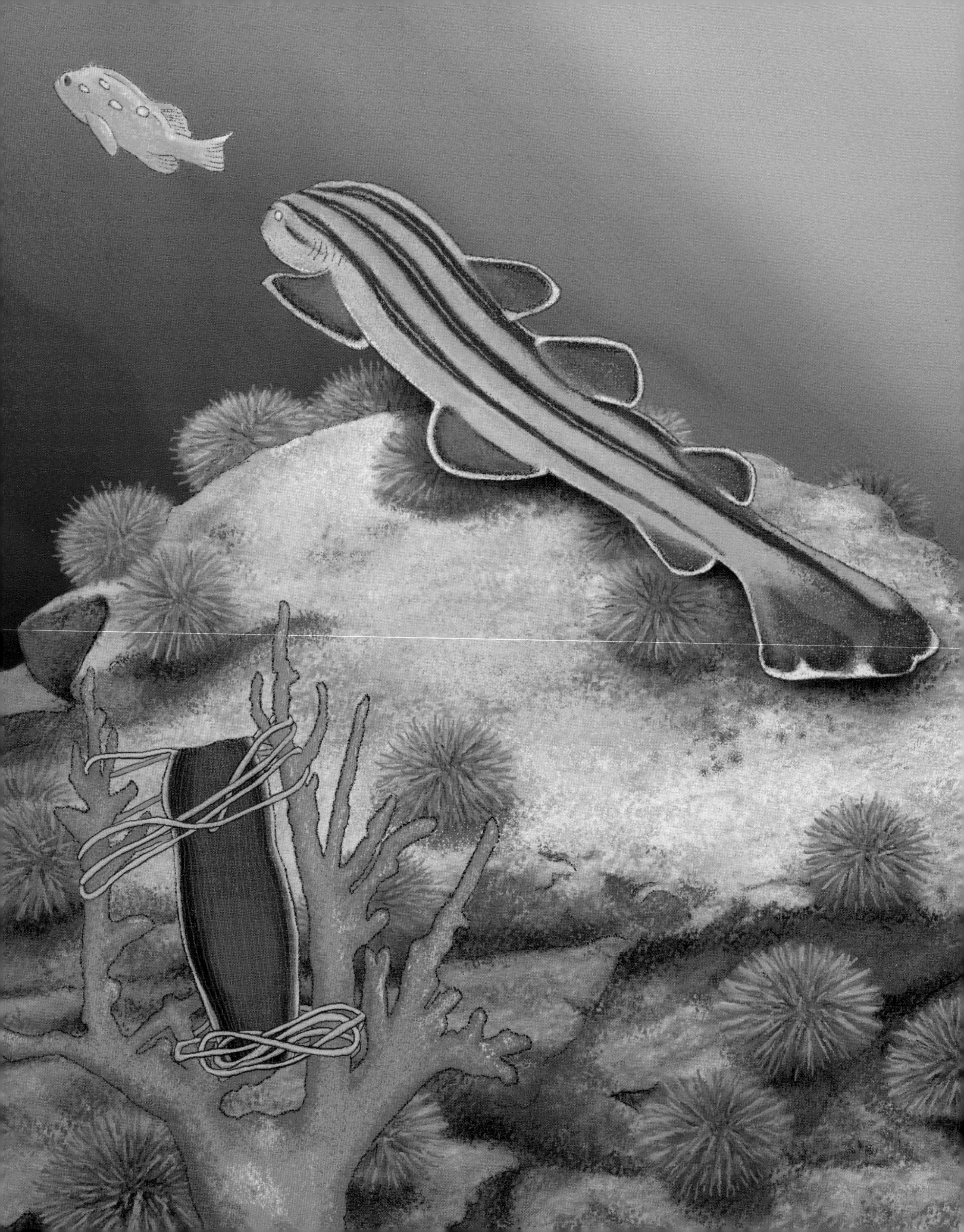

But the pajama shark just scoffed. "Your case is all weathered and worn. You can't be a pajama shark, not with an egg case like that," he said. And he sped off, chasing a fish over the rocky reef.

Maybe I am the only creature like me in the whole wide ocean, thought Shark Baby. The thought made him feel very lonely and small.

Then, Shark Baby heard a deep voice.

"You need to talk to the mermaid," it said.

Mama Octopus was looking at Shark Baby from the entrance to her cave.

"How can the mermaid help?" asked Shark Baby.

"Because you are the mermaid's purse," said the octopus. "She will know what you are and where you belong."

"Can you take me to her?" asked Shark Baby.

"No, I must care for my babies," said the octopus, and Shark Baby saw her thousand and one children, hanging from the ceiling of the cave in pearly strands.

Shark Baby didn't know what the mermaid was, or how to find her.

But Mother Ocean picked that baby up in her arms one last time, oh, so gently, and carried him by moonlight through the shadowy sea and finally set him down in a watery meadow in another ocean. The mermaid (who was really a manatee) was munching seagrass.

"Are you the mermaid?" Shark Baby asked shyly.

"If you are a near-sighted sailor I am!" said the manatee. "I suppose someone told you that you were a mermaid's purse."

"Yes," said Shark Baby. "They did."

"Look at me," said the manatee, "and tell me if you are big enough to be a pocketbook for a mermaid the size of me!"

“But where do I belong?” wailed Shark Baby.

“I think I know,” said the manatee. And she called over a manta ray, and told him to take Shark Baby back to the green, striped world where the seahorses play.

And the ray curled Shark Baby under his wing and swam with him, right back to his own little patch of the kelp forest.

It wasn't a moment too soon—the tattered egg case split wide open and Shark Baby slipped into the cool water.

But a young sea lion was there to greet him, with his mouth of big, sharp teeth!

Shark Baby puffed himself up until he was twice his size and scared the sea lion away.

“Whoa!” said a voice. “You looked just like Old Man Pufferfish when you did that.”

Shark Baby let out all the water he’d gulped and turned to see a small shark.

“You’re kind of tiny. What kind of shark are you?”

The new shark puffed himself up until he was twice as big, too.

“A swell shark, silly! Just like you. Want to play?”

As they raced off together into the kelp forest, Shark Baby thought, “A swell shark is a very swell thing to be!”

For Creative Minds

The For Creative Minds educational section may be photocopied or printed from our website by the owner of this book for educational, non-commercial uses. Cross-curricular teaching activities, interactive quizzes, and more are available online. Go to www.SylvanDellPublishing.com and click on the book's cover to explore all the links.

Sharks

Fish come in all different shapes, colors, and sizes. Some fishes have hard bones as we do.

Other fishes, like sharks and rays, don't have any hard bones at all! Their skeletons are made up of cartilage—the same stuff that forms our noses and ears.

Sharks get their oxygen from the water through gills.

Sharks usually live in saltwater (marine) habitats. While some sharks swim up rivers, they do not normally live in lakes.

Many sharks are crepuscular, meaning they hunt at dawn and dusk. If swimming in the ocean, it is best to stay out of the water at that time.

Some sharks eat fish, seals, sea lions, and even whales. Some sharks eat plankton! Others, like the swell sharks, eat clams and crabs.

Contrary to what many people believe, sharks do not hunt humans. Shark attacks are usually sharks "checking out" what food might be available. Or, like many other animals, they may attack people if they feel threatened.

Sharks may be at the top of the ocean food web, but humans are their biggest predators.

Because millions of sharks are killed by human fishing, fewer survive to adulthood to have babies of their own.

Some sharks are big
and some are small.

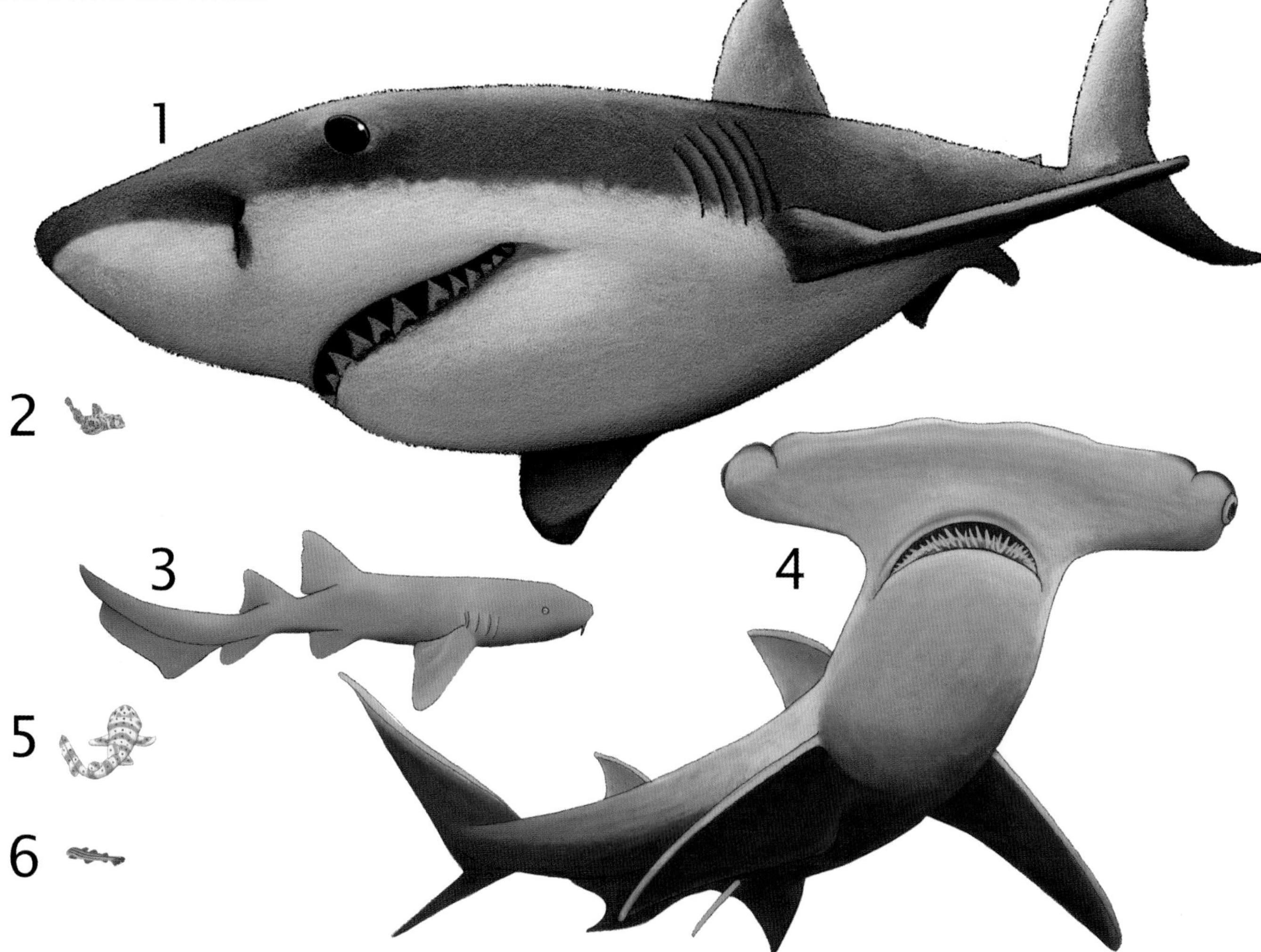

1. Great white sharks often "test-bite" unfamiliar objects, such as buoys, flotsam, surfboards, or strange prey, in order to identify them.
2. Horn sharks sometimes stand on their heads to pry prey loose from underwater rocks.
3. During the day, nurse sharks can be found resting in groups, tucking themselves into crevices or under overhangs in the reef. They leave the group to hunt alone at night.
4. Hammerhead sharks have a special sensory organ under their "hammer" that can detect electric fields. This helps the shark find prey hiding behind rocks or under sand.
5. To escape danger, swell sharks puff themselves up with water so they are twice their size. This makes it harder for predators to bite or pull swell sharks from rocky holes.
6. Pajama sharks (also called striped catsharks) are dressed for bed. They spend their days sleeping in rock crevices or among kelp and hunt at night.

Compare and Contrast Egg Cases

Birds, most reptiles, many insects, and even sharks and other fish hatch from eggs! Bird mothers build nests and care for their eggs and young. Many other animals lay eggs and leave. The young will hatch and then survive on instinct.

Sharks, skates, and rays are all "cousins." Some sharks hatch from eggs inside their mothers' bodies. Rays and some sharks give birth to live young. Other sharks and skates lay egg cases that are often found on beaches. The cases, nicknamed "mermaid purses," remain tough and rubbery long after the pups hatch.

Some shark egg cases have long, thin structures (tendrils) that attach to an object.

Egg cases can be tough and rubbery, like a shark egg case, or rigid and hard, like a bird's egg shell. Both protect the unhatched animals growing inside.

How are these egg cases alike and how are they different?

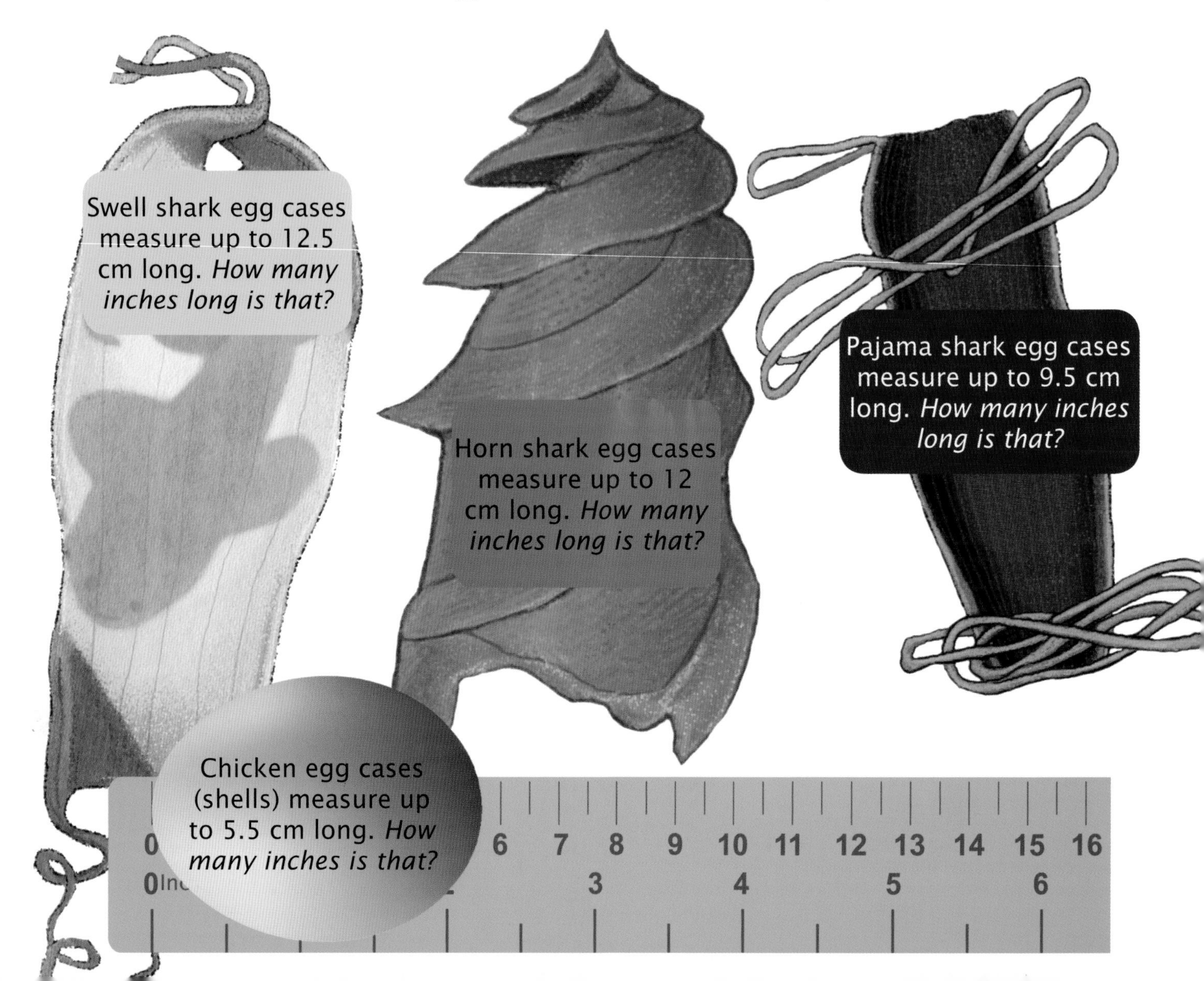

Sharks True or False?

Do you think these shark statements are true or false? Answers are upside-down, below.

1. Sharks are bloodthirsty, man-eating killers.
2. All sharks are powerful hunters with big, sharp teeth.
3. Sharks are mindless eating machines.
4. Sharks have to keep swimming to breathe.
5. When you see a fin sticking out of the water, it's a shark.
6. Sharks have teeth on their skin.
7. Sharks are a serious danger to people.
8. Sharks have superpowers.
9. Sharks live in every ocean of the world.
10. Sharks need your help.

1) False! Humans are not sharks' natural prey and most accidents are cases of mistaken identity.

2) False! It's true that many sharks are top predators (animals that prey on animals). But there are many different kinds of sharks, not all of them have big, sharp teeth. The whale shark is a gentle giant that filters tiny plants and animals (plankton) from the ocean. The Port Jackson shark has bony plates in its mouth to crush clams and crabs.

3) False! While it's hard to study sharks in the lab, we know they have large brains. Many aquariums have trained their sharks to feed from specific targets. They may need those large brains to cope with life in the ocean and their dealings with other sharks. Scientists are working to learn more about what goes on in shark brains.

4) True and false! Sharks breathe when oxygen in seawater passes over their gills. Most sharks need to swim to keep water flowing through their gills. But some sharks have special structures that pump water over their gills while resting on the ocean floor.

5) False! Fins above the surface could belong to dolphins, whales, or even sailfish.

6) True! Sharks are covered in tiny tooth-like scales called denticles. Denticles give their sharkskin its rough, sandpapery feel.

7) False. Humans kill tens of millions of sharks every year just for their fins to make shark-fin soup. Millions more sharks die when they are caught in fishing nets or when we grind them up into useless pills to "cure" cancer. In 2011, only 75 people around the world were bitten by sharks and 12 died. Sharks have more to fear from us than we have to fear from them!

8) True! Sharks have senses that we humans don't share, kind of like shark superpowers. Just as the superhero Spider-Man™ has spider sense, sharks have a special shark sense that helps them detect the faint electrical signals given off by their prey. They have good hearing and a great sense of smell, too.

9) True! Sharks are found from tropical reefs to cold, polar oceans. But they tend to be found in special places within each ocean where they find what they need to eat and have baby sharks.

10) True! Sharks have been swimming Earth's oceans for millions of years, but some species are in danger of going extinct like the dinosaurs.

To Wren, for her friendship and inspiration. Thanks to Harry Breidahl of the Marine Education Society of Australia for supplying actual shark egg cases for me to examine—AD

While doing research for the illustrations, I visited the New England Aquarium in Boston, MA; swam with the manatees of Crystal River, FL; and visited the Monterey Bay Aquarium in Monterey, CA; the California Academy of Sciences; and the Aquarium of The Bay—both in San Francisco, CA. I especially want to thank Captain Ché Ruble and his wife, Katie, for providing me with their own manatee photos after the water was too murky for me to get my own, Jim Fuller at the Monterey Bay Aquarium, Nan Sincero at the California Academy of Sciences, and Ora Zolan at the Aquarium of The Bay. Once again, none of these adventures would be possible without the support of my loving family. Muchas gracias—SB

Thanks to Jason Robertshaw and the education staff at Mote Marine for verifying the accuracy of the information in this book.

Library of Congress Cataloging-in-Publication Data
Downer, Ann, 1960-
Shark baby / by Ann Downer ; illustrated by Shennen Bersani.
p. cm.
Summary: A shark, still in his egg case, sets out to determine what kind of shark he is.
ISBN 978-1-60718-622-9 (English hardcover) -- ISBN 978-1-60718-709-7 (Spanish hardcover) -- ISBN 978-1-60718-634-2 (English pbk.) -- ISBN 978-1-60718-646-5 (English ebook (downloadable)) -- ISBN 978-1-60718-658-8 (Spanish ebook (downloadable)) -- ISBN 978-1-60718-670-0 (interactive English/Spanish ebook (web-based)) [1. Sharks--Fiction. 2. Animals--Infancy--Fiction. 3. Identity--Fiction. 4. Marine animals--Fiction.]
I. Bersani, Shennen, ill. II. Title.
PZ7.D7575Sh 2013
[E]--dc23

012033707

Shark Baby: Original Title in English
El tiburoncito: Spanish Title

Lexile® Level: 700L
key phrases for educators: life cycle, ocean habitats, adaptations, anthropomorphic, compare/contrast

Manufactured in China, December 2012
This product conforms to CPSIA 2008
First Printing

Sylvan Dell Publishing
Mt. Pleasant, SC 29464
www.SylvanDellPublishing.com